Washington Irving, Dudley Buck

The Legend of Don Munio

A Dramatic Cantata

Washington Irving, Dudley Buck

The Legend of Don Munio
A Dramatic Cantata

ISBN/EAN: 9783337375782

Printed in Europe, USA, Canada, Australia, Japan

Cover: Foto ©Andreas Hilbeck / pixelio.de

More available books at **www.hansebooks.com**

THE

LEGEND OF DON MUNIO.

A

DRAMATIC CANTATA.

WORDS AND MUSIC

By

DUDLEY BUCK.

Op. 62.

BOSTON:
PUBLISHED BY OLIVER DITSON & COMPANY.
NEW-YORK: C. H. DITSON & CO.—CHICAGO: LYON & HEALY.

CHARACTERS REPRESENTED.

Don Munio de Hinojosa...BASS.

Donna Maria—his wife......................................SOPRANO.

Escobedo—chaplain to Don Munio.......................BARITONE.

Abadil—a Moorish prince..................................TENOR.

Constanza—his betrothed........................... MEZZO SOPR. OR CONTRALTO.

Roderigo—a messenger. ....TENOR.

Chorus of Huntsmen, Retainers, and Female Dependents,
   both Spanish and Moorish.

Scene, a border castle. Time, of the Spanish and Moorish Wars.

The versification of the libretto is made from the "Spanish Papers" of Washington Irving.

N. B. The orchestral parts to this Work may be obtained through the Publishers. Choral societies may also obtain an edition comprising the *Choruses only*. The following numbers may be had singly in sheet form :—

   No. 2. RECIT. AND ARIA (Soprano) " Within my chamber."
   No. 5. " " " (Bass) " In circle wide."
   No. 12. " " " (Tenor) " The shadows deepen."
   No. 14. DUET (Mezzo Soprano and Tenor) " Dews of the Summer night."
   No. 17. QUARTET, (without Accompt.) " It is the lot of friends to part."
   Also the Overture and Bolero for Piano four hands.

THE LEGEND OF DON MUNIO.

·

OVERTURE.

No. 1.—CHORUS OF HONTSMEN AND RETAINERS.

Early morning. Court yard of Don Munio's castle.

To the field! to the hunt! ye men one and all!
See the East with rosy tints gleaming !
Soon Aurora's bright rays on our weapons will fall,
No battle, no feud doth to-day on us call ;
To the field, to the hunt, then, ye brave warriors all,
No time now for sloth or for dreaming.

Ere the rays of the sun shall dispel the night-dew,
From his couch the noble stag wakening,
With steed and with hound will we keep him in view,
Till he fall, a fair prize to our arrow so true ;
To horse, then. to horse! ere is gone the night dew,
To the field, to the hunt we are hastening.

And if, midst the chase, we should chance on the foe,
Should near us the Moslem be hiding,
Of strong arms and sharp swords make we here goodly show,
In the dust shall the infidel host be laid low!
Through God, and our leader, who dreads not the foe,
Every danger and fear thus deriding.
To the field, to the hunt, &c.

No. 2.—RECITATIVE AND ARIA. (Soprano.)

*The Castle of Don Munio. Donna Maria alone in her chamber.
Toward sunset.*

RECIT. (a.)
Within my chamber, wrapt in silent musing,
Oppressed with loneliness I sit forlorn.
Now slowly sinks the sun towards the glowing west,
The shadows lengthen, and the birds fly home.

ARIA.
O heart, my heart, expand thy pinions!
And like the birds, soar far away ;
Not here, not here are thy dominions,
But near thy lord—there wouldst thou stay.

O absence, absence ! source of sorrow,
To her thus doomed to watch and wait,
None can foretell howe'er the morrow
With joy or grief may change our state.

RECIT. (b)
But why should I thus gloomy ponder ?
Will not a gracious Heaven protect!
Hath not my lord full oft returned
After repeated absence?

ARIA. (*allegro.*)
Then cheer thee, my heart! why shouldst thou repine ?
To the field the brave warrior must go ;
And patiently waiting, seek not to divine
What the future will speedily show.

In chivalrous bearing, in knightly address,
What warrior more honora can claim ?
All powerful in combat, most kind in distress,
My own liege—how I cherish thy fame!

Then banish the thought! my own noble knight
Shall return in despite of the foe.
What joy when afar his loved form greets my sight,
And his bugles their welcome shall blow!

No. 3.—THE RESPONSES AND ARIETTA.

*Evening. The chapel of the castle. Escobedo, the chaplain, with
the women, and such retainers as have not followed their
master on his expedition. Conclusion of the vesper service.*

ESCOBEDO.
Gloria Patri et Filio, et Spiritui Sancto!

CHORUS.
*Sicut erat in principio, et nunc et semper,
Et in sæcula sæculorum. Amen !*

ESCOBEDO.
Pax vobiscum.

CHORUS.
Et eum Spiritu tuo.

RECIT.
ESCOBEDO.
The night hath fallen round us ;
We have prayed for our good lord and lady ;
Yet ere we part, as is most meet and right,
And as enjoined by Holy Church,
Our voices let us raise in Vesper Song.

ARIETTA.
All other thoughts forsake,
Let each his station take,
Let holy song awake
In accents sweet.

To her let praise be given,
Who for our sins hath striven,
Who, that we be forgiven,
Doth plead for us.
Ave Maria !

No. 4.—CHORUS.

Ave Maria ! full of grace!
Mother of sorrows, bow thine ear ;
Withhold not thou thy kindly face,
Our supplications deign to hear.
Ave Maria !

Benedicta ! blessèd maid!
Chosen of women fair and pure,
Support our hearts when sore dismayed,
Let not the world our souls allure.
Ave Maria !

Et Benedictus ! wondrous birth
Of Christ our Lord of virgin pure!
Through Him salvation came to earth,
Through thee His aid is ever sure.
Ave Maria !

In hora mortis ! when the hour
Of death shall come, our troubles past,
O pray for us that by the power
Of grace we may be saved at last.
Ora pro nobis peccatoribus !

No. 5.—RECITATIVE AND ARIA. (Bass.)

Morning in the Forest. Don Munio alone.

RECIT.

In circle wide forth have I sent my vassals all.
Aroused by loud halloh and blast of horn,
Ere long the frighted stag hither his flight will wend ;
While 'neath this leafy covert will I take my stand,
Expectant waiting till the game appear.

In the woods at early morn
Sweet resound the forest voices,
Nature seems again new-born,
And the heart of man rejoices.
How the forest odors sweet
Breathe their perfumes on the air!
Blest influence! thee my soul doth greet,
Soother of sorrow and of care.

Strong of arm and cool of nerve
Must the trusty warrior be.
Huntsmen! thou, too, must not swerve
When the game approacheth thee.
Worthy then of knightly skill
Is the sport the woods can show,
When peals the horn from cliff and hill,
And echo answers faint below.

No. 6.—RECITATIVE.—DON MUNIO.

But hark! what distant sounds of music fall on my wondering ear.
In yonder vale, behold a cavalcade approaching, and women too
Among the train, all gaily decked as for a wedding feast.
No hostile purpose can their footsteps guide, while yet their
Glittering garb proclaims the Moslem! Ha! my good sword!
Here shalt thou wie both noble booty and a lordly ransom.
Sound! bugle, sound ! with gladsome news my vassals to recall.

No. 7.—CHORUS. (Female Voices.)

Strains of a Moorish march. Females of the Moorish cavalcade singing as they journey.

Birds gaily singing o'er us,
Haste on the path before us,
Raising the joyous chorus,
In praise of Love.
Ere fall the shades of night,
O may the marriage rite
Two faithful hearts unite,
Sing praise to Love.

O may kind Heaven defend,
Until our journey end,
Freely our songs we spend
In praise of Love.
Thus safe from every ill,
Our good lord, Abadil
In peace shall journey still,
And win the prize.

No. 8.—CHORUS.

Don Munio's retainers make their appearance from all sides, wholly surrounding the Moors. Ensemble.

DON MUNIO'S FOLLOWERS.

Down with the Moslem! the hated—detested!
No longer shall thus our fair land be infested ;
On warriors all! draw the sword! bend the bow!
For God and Castile! see yonder the foe!

THE MOORISH WOMEN.

Woe ! woe! utter woe! our journey detected,
By blood-thirsty men is our progress arrested.
All the hopes fondly raised, in the dust are laid low,
And captives are we to our bitterest foe.

DON MUNIO.

Captured the Moslem ! the hated—detested!
The spoil—it is ours—by our good swords arrested !
We war not with women—each weapon lay low !
What rejoicing at home when this booty we show !

ABADIL AND CONSTANZA.

Woe ! woe ! utter woe ! etc.

ALL.

Surrounded !
Confounded !
No succor.
No rescue.

To whom } can { we } turn !
none } they

No. 9.—RECIT. AND ARIA.—ABADIL.

Unarmed, we yield ourselves to force of numbers.
But heard I not, amidst yon hostile cries,
The name of Munio ?

DON MUNIO.

'Tis even so—the knight who speaks with you is he,
What wouldst thou ?

ABADIL.—"THE ENTREATY."

Hail, O noble Munio!
On me a boon bestow,
Known as a generous foe
To thee I plead.
Do not my suit disown
When once our purpose known,
In thee I trust alone
To help our need.

My name is Abadil—of princely line,
And this fair maid of equal high descent,
To celebrate our marriage at a distant shrine,
Thither had we this day our footsteps bent.
Take all our gold, our jewels rich and rare
The ransom of a prince—aye ! ask for more,
But let not fell dishonor have a share,
In what sad Fate may have for us in store.
Then, O noble Munio! etc.

DON MUNIO'S RETAINERS.

(whispering together during the latter part of Abadil's Aria.)

The bride is passing fair,
Witness her great despair !
List to the warrior's tale !
The story seemeth true,
What will Don Munio do?
Can aught avail ?

No. 10.—RECIT. AND INTERMEZZO. — "THE RANSOM."

Now God forbid that I, a Christian Knight,
Two loving hearts should force asunder ;
Though with no hostile purpose ye have come,
But yet as Moslems captives of my sword,
Hear this, the ransom I will take.

Full fourteen days within my castle-gate
Captive, yet not confined, shall ye abide with me,
But there your nuptials will we celebrate,
After which time shall ye indeed go free.
Haste, herald, haste, unto my lady fair!
That for our coming she at once prepare.

No. 11.—GENERAL CHORUS OF MOORS AND CHRISTIANS.

Praise to Don Munio!
What kindness to his foe
Doth the brave warrior show!
Let joy abound.

ABADIL AND CONSTANZA.

Away with grief and fear!
All sorrows disappear,
Such Knighthood we revere
Where'er 'tis found.

CHORUS.

Sound, trumpets, sound! the bridal train preceding,
Sound, gentle lutes! Your tale of love revealing,
Haste on your way, your banners wide displaying,
To Hymen's feast let there be no delaying.
Praise to Don Munio! etc.

END OF PART I.

PART II.

No. 12.—RECIT. AND ARIA.—ABADIL.

The day preceding the nuptials. A terrace of Don Munio's castle. Sunset. Abadil awaiting Constanza.

The shadows deepen on the castle walls ;
Honored captivity draws near its close.
Soon will the Christian Even-Song
Proclaim the coming of the night,
While on this terrace will I wait
    To meet my love.
Patience, O longing heart! soon is thy trial o'er ;
And the glad morrow's sun shall see Constanza thine!

O thou, my star in darkening night!
  O thou, my light to guide my way!
My joy when all around seems bright,
  My comfort in the threatening day.

For thee my heart is ever longing,
  With love's own grief full sore opprest ;
I think of thee—and tears come thronging,
  When thou art present I am blest.

Waft her, O breeze, my tend'rest greeting ;
  I hear the chant from chapel near,
The hour draws nigh for our glad meeting,
  O come, sweet love, I'm waiting here.

No. 13.—CHORUS.

The chapel choir chanting the Evening-Hymn.

"JESU, DULCIS MEMORIA."—(Translation.)

Jesu, how sweet the very thought,
That Thou our hearts true joy hast brought,
Honey in sweetness is as naught
To that with which Thy presence fraught.

Jesu, the hope of penitent!
How free to us Thy grace is spent!
Ah ! who can doubt Thy kind intent
To souls which Thee to seek are bent.

O Jesu! evermore with Thee,
Be our reward Thy face to see,
And, thro' a bright eternity,
Thine shall for aye the glory be. Amen.

No. 14.—DUETT.

Night. The terrace of the castle. The Moorish lovers.

ABADIL AND CONSTANZA.

Dews of the summer-night gently are falling,
Kindly the stars look down from on high ;
Hark in the grove to the nightingale calling!
We are alone—no listener is nigh.

ABADIL.

Constanza! my loved one! my bride on the morrow!
Glide swift fleeting hours till the dawn shall appear!
Dispelled are the clouds which but now threatened sorrow,
The bright sun of Hope hath removed every fear.

CONSTANZA.

Dearest! my dearest! my thoughts art thou telling ;
O welcome the morrow which makes me thy bride!
These tears from mine eyes which now gently are welling,
But show forth the joy which I feel at thy side.

BOTH.

Then while the night-dews gently are falling,
While kindly stars the deep azure adorn,
Hie we to rest—soon cometh the morning,
Farewell, love, farewell!—until the glad morn.

No. 15.—CHORUS.

(The Festivities following the marriage)

United! United!
  Their sorrows requited,
Behold the happy pair advance!
United! United!
  All are invited
To join the maze of the merry dance.

FEMALE VOICES.

Lead on, lead on in merry, merry dance,
This joyous day should every soul entrance,
Sing, sing, in happy measure show
The love we bear Don Munio.

MALE VOICES.

Safe through life—secure from ill,
Guard, gracious Heaven, the noble Abadil ;
May joy his wedded state attend,
Crowned with rich blessings to life's end.
United! United! etc.

No. 16—BOLERO, FOR ORCHESTRA.

No. 17.—QUARTETT.—(Unaccompanied.)

The departure of the Moors.

DON MUNIO, DONNA MARIA, ABADIL AND CONSTANZA.

It is the lot of friends to part,
We meet as travellers of a day,
An interchange of heart we start,
And then each turns and goes his way.

O, human life! how short thou art,
The joys of friendship well to learn!
No sooner prized than forced apart ;
How hard God's purpose to discern.

And thus we part—we cannot know
How we again perchance may meet,
Whether opposed as foe to foe,
Or as a friend his friend doth greet.

Then, meantime, let us hope and trust
That this our friendship may endure,
May all our purposes be just,
And thus their due reward secure.
Farewell, kind friends, farewell!

No. 18.—DUETT.

A Chamber in the castle. Don Munio and Donna Maria.

DON MUNIO.

Once more my royal master's call,
Throughout the land by herald sped,
Summons to him his warriors all,
Again must Moslem blood be shed.

DONNA MARIA.

O direful tidings! must thou go?
Again from wife and home depart ?
O cruel war! what bitter woe
Thou bringest to my anxious heart.

DON MUNIO.

Stern duty calls ; I must obey!
Though now I feel th' approach of age:
This once—and then with thee I'll stay,
With tend'rest love thy cares assuage.

DONNA MARIA.

O wilt thou promise?

DON MUNIO.

Aye, indeed!
But once more would I then forsake.

DONNA MARIA.

Ah why?

DON MUNIO.

That to the Holy Land
A pilgrimage I then might make.

BOTH.

Soon may the Moslem conquered be,
Then shall sweet Peace descend,
And o'er our land, from foes made free,
Dire War shall have an end.

DON MUNIO.

Yes, I must go! his sov'reign's call
Each knight should swift obey,
Far better like a warrior fall
Than craven here to stay.

DONNA MARIA.

Yes, thou must go! thy sov'reign's call
I know thou shouldst obey,
Far better like a warrior fall,
Than craven here to stay.

No. 19.—BATTLE HYMN. (Male voices.)

The courtyard of the Castle. Gathering of Don Munio's Retainers.

Bring forth the clashing spear and shield!
To-day we seek the battle field,
Before us make the foe to yield,
   Great God of Battle!

And if it be our doom to lie
Outstretched beneath some sullen sky,
Receive our souls to Thee on high,
   Great God of Battle!

Or if the victory duly won
'Neath Palestine's resplendent sun,
The pilgrim-staff we'll bear.
   This we swear!

The Sepulchre of our dear Lord,
That spot of all on earth adored,
To seek, be our first care;
   This we swear!

Then teach us how to choose the right,
Thine is the victory, power and might,
Through Thee alone we win the fight,
   Great God of Battle!

No. 20.—CHORUS.

The chapel of the Castle. Choir chanting the dirge for the dead.

   Requiem aeternam Domini!
   Dona eis requiem,
   Et lux perpetua luceat eis!

No. 21.—ESCOBEDO, WITH CHORUS.

The chaplain addresses those assembled.

A year hath passed this very day
Since our good Knight did wend his way
To meet the Moslem host.
Ye know the tale so full of woe,
How many a noble head lay low,
And his life, too, was lost.

CHORUS. (*Sotto voce.*)

Alas! his life was lost!

ESCOBEDO.

'Twas passing strange that thus his end
Should come by hand of former friend,
   The noble Abdil.
With vizor closed, all shining steel,
Naught did at first the fact reveal
   That Munio was dead.

CHORUS. (*Sotto voce.*)

Don Munio was dead!

ESCOBEDO.

Fruitless the grief of noble foe,
Fruitless the widow's tears and woe,
   For now 'twas all in vain!
With frequent masses for his soul,
O may he soon attain the goal
   Of heavenly bliss above.

Now while we thus assembled are,
A messenger hath come from far
   A wondrous tale to tell!

Give heed, and list with bated breath,
Give heed, and learn how e'en in death
   A knightly pledge fulfilled.

CHORUS.

What can these words presage?
Right gladly we engage
   Attention strict to give.

No. 22.—RODERIGO. *The message from Palestine.*

RECIT.

Full many a long and weary league,
From Palestine, the sacred land, I come.
Jerusalem, the Holy City,
One year ago a sight most strange beheld;
To make it known to you am I commissioned.

ARIA.

One summer eve, as sank the sun,
While vesper-bells to prayer did call,
Full seventy warriors—one by one,
Drew near the Holy Sepulchre!

All deadly pale, with vizor raised
In silence moved their steady march,
The crowd stood wondering, and gazed
Towards the Holy Sepulchre!

But I myself full well did know
The leader of this knightly band,
It was your own Don Munio
Approached the Holy Sepulchre!

CHORUS. (*Excitedly but sotto voce,*)

What do we hear! Can this be true
Don Munio was seen by you!

RODERIGO.

They knelt within in silent prayer
After the sacred gates were passed,
Then faded into empty air
Within the Holy Sepulchre!

Rejoice that thus their vow fulfilled,
Even in death their honor proved,
Thus it took place, as God had willed
Before the Holy Sepulchre!

No. 23.—CHORUS. FINALE.

In thankful hymns ascending,
Let all their voices raise,
Jehovah! All protecting!
Accept our grateful praise.

Through Thee their combats ended,
Through Thee fulfilled their vow,
Their honor, safe defended,
Is crowned with victory now.

   Glory eternal,
   Rapture supernal,
   Bliss never ending,
   Now hath begun;
   Passed the bright portals,
   Seraphs immortal
   Praises are singing,
   Heaven is won!
Alleluia! Alleluia! Alleluia!
   Amen!

CONTENTS.

PART I.

OVERTURE.

DUDLEY BUCK. Op. 62.

No. 1. Chorus of Huntsmen and Retainers.

"To the field, to the hunt!"

Early morning. The Court-yard of Don Munio's castle.

all! With ro - sy tint be - hold the East is gleam - - - -

ing! Soon Au - ro - ra's bright rays on our weap-ons will fall,

A No bat - tle, no feud doth to-day on us

pel the night-dew From his couch the noble stag a - wak' - ning, With steed and with hound will we

keep him in view, Till he fall a fair prize to our arrow so true; To horse, then! to

horse! ere is gone the nightdew. To the field, to the hunt we are hast' - - ning.

O

Or if, midst the chase, we chance on the

foe, Should near us the Mos - lem be hid . . . .

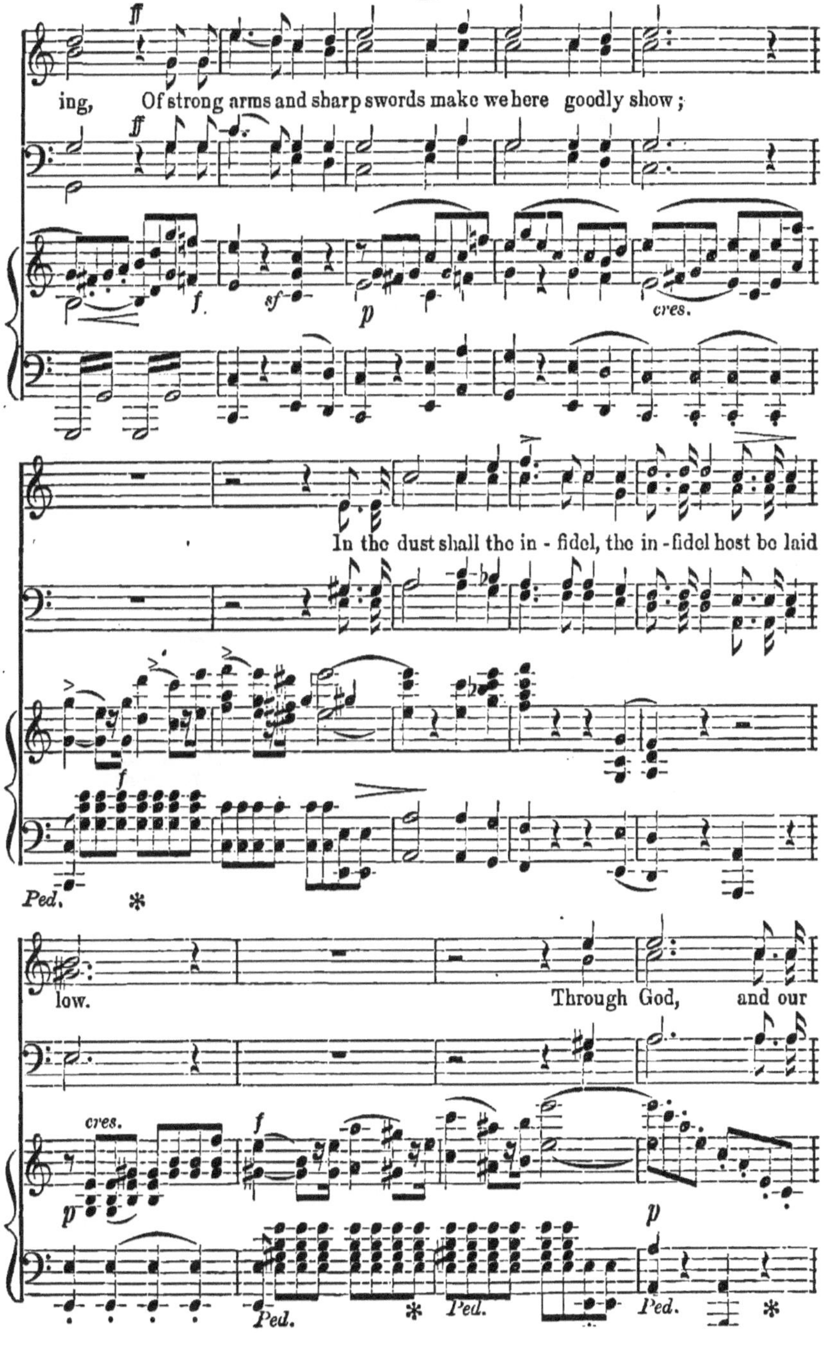

ing,   Of strong arms and sharp swords make we here goodly show;

In the dust shall the in - fidel, the in - fidel host be laid

low.   Through God,   and our

loud or who dreads not the foe, All dan-ger and fear thus de-

rid - - ing. To horse! then to horse! ere is

gone the nightdew, While with ro-sy tints the East is gleam-ing. Soon Au-ro - ra's bright rays on our

weapons shall fall. No bat - tle, no feud doth to-day on us call, No time, no

energico.

time now, no time now for sloth or for dream · ing. To the

field! to the field! . . . .

No. 2. Recitative and Aria. "Within my chamber."

The castle of Don Munio. Sunset. Donna Maria alone in her chamber.

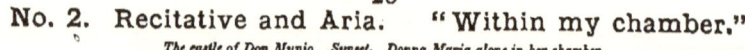

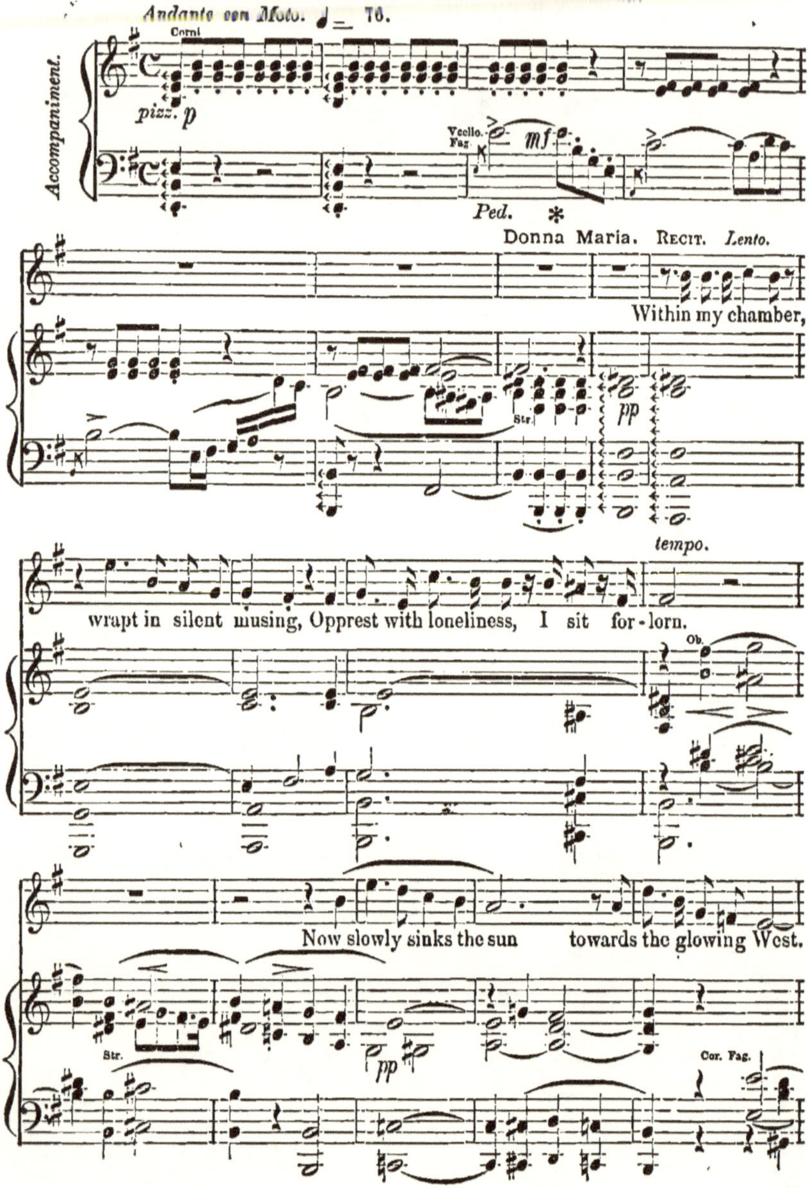

Andante con Moto. ♩ = 76.
Accompaniment.
Corni
pizz. p
Vcello. Fag.
mf
Ped. *
Str.
Donna Maria. Recit. Lento.
pp
Within my chamber,
wrapt in silent musing, Opprest with loneliness, I sit for-lorn.
tempo.
Ob.
Str.
pp
Cor. Fag.
Now slowly sinks the sun towards the glowing West.

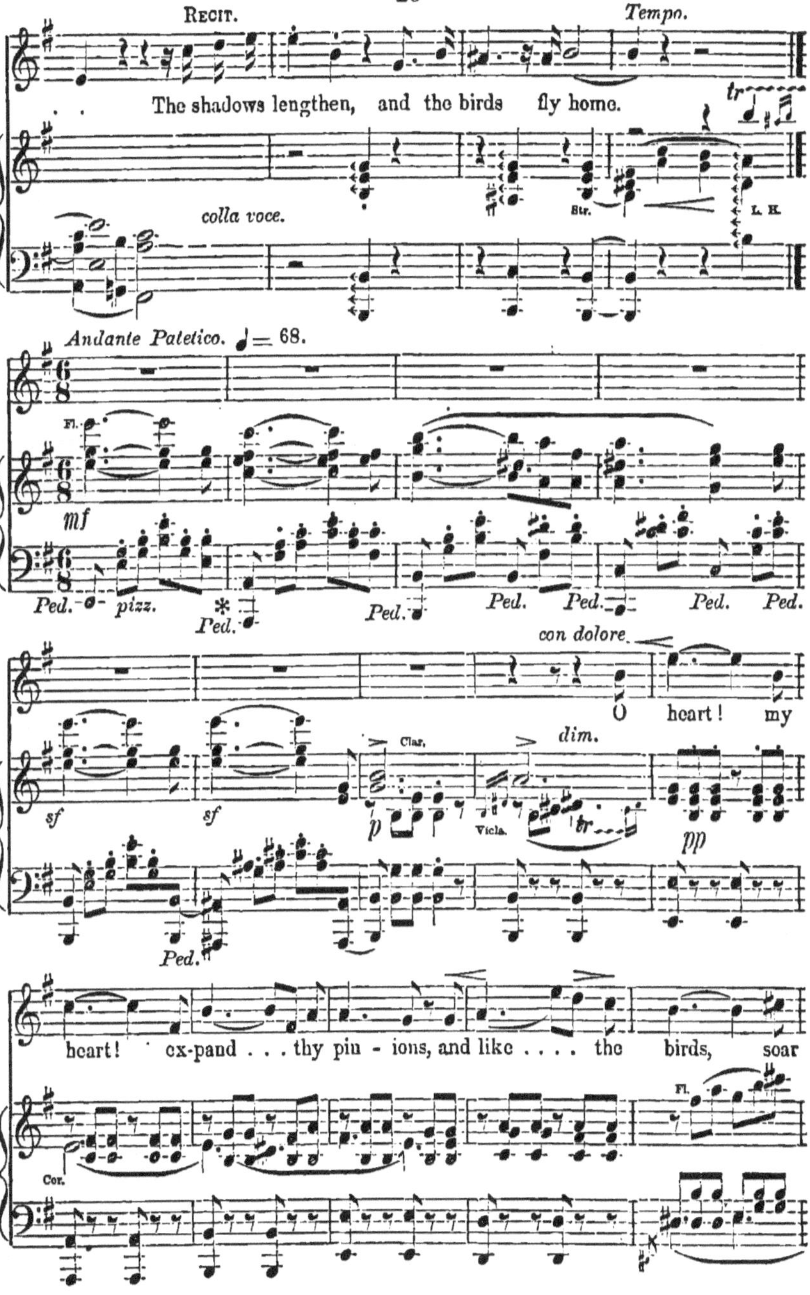
RECIT.
Tempo.
The shadows lengthen, and the birds fly home.
tr
colla voce.
Str.
L. H.
Andante Patetico. ♩= 68.
Fl.
mf
Ped. pizz.
Ped.
Ped.
Ped.
Ped.
Ped.
Ped.
con dolore
O heart! my
Clar.
dim.
sf
sf
p
Viola.
tr
pp
Ped.
heart! ex-pand . . . thy pin - ions, and like . . . . the birds, soar
Fl.
Cor.

far . . . . a = way! . . Not here, not here, not here are thy do -

min - ions, But near thy lord, . . . there wouldst thou stay.

O ab - sence,

ab - sence! source of sor - row, To her thus doom'd to watch, to

mor - row, With joy ... or grief may change our state, With

joy ... or grief ... may change ..... our state, ...

RECIT. *Vivace.*

But why should I thus gloomy ponder? Will not a gracious Heav'n pro-

- tect? Hath not my lord full oft returned,

mf Wind Inst. *pizz.* Str. *p*

lento.

after repeated ab - sence? Then

Vivace. f *sf*

cheer thee, my heart, Why should'st thou repine? To the field the brave warrior must

Clar

p

Allegro ma non Troppo. ♩ = 116.

go! And pa - tient-ly wait - ing, Seek not to di-vine what the

fu - ture shall speed - i - ly show, Then cheer thee, my heart, Why

should'st thou repine? To the field the brave warrior must go! And

pa - tient-ly waiting, seek not to divine What the future shall speed - i - ly

show. In chiv - al - rous bearing, In knight - ly ad - dress, What war - rior more hon - ors, more hon - ors can claim! All - power - ful in combat, most kind in distress, O my liege! my

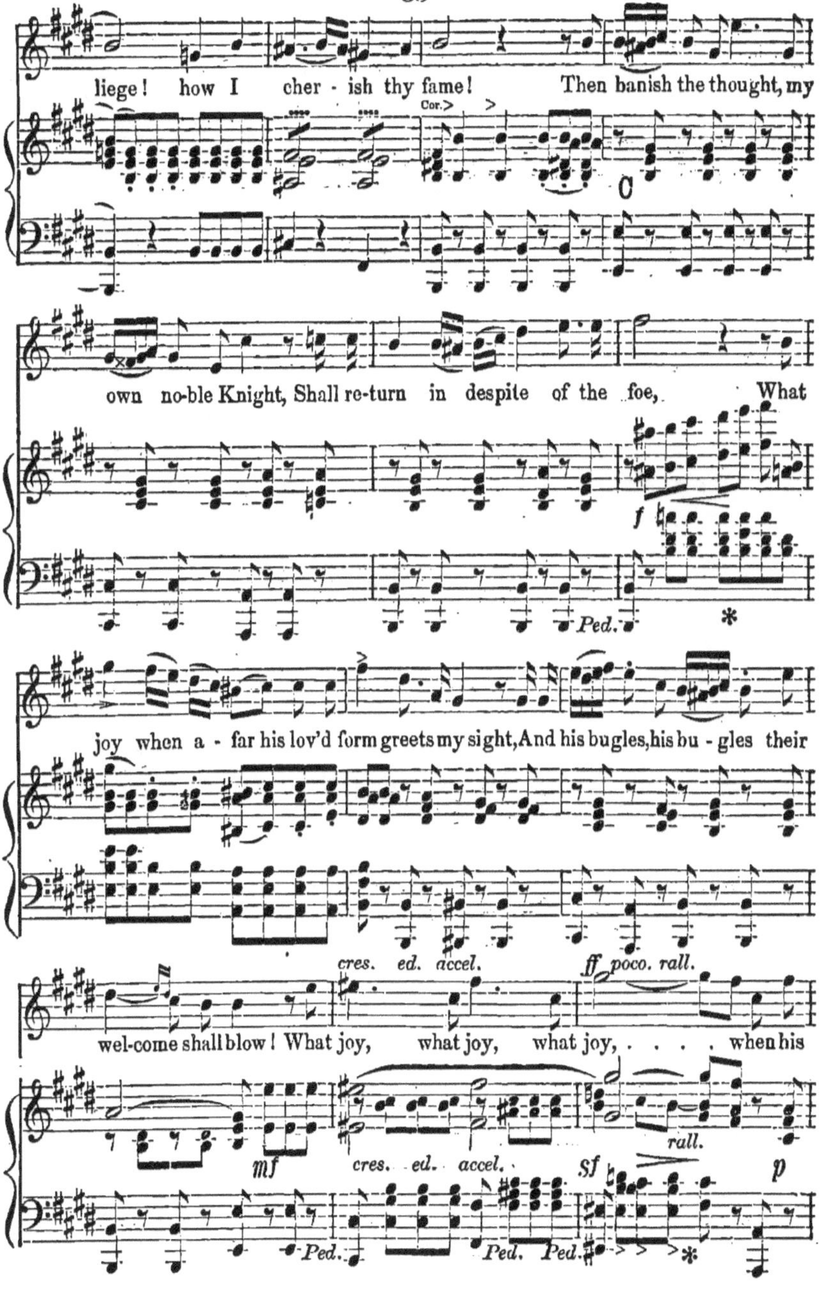
liege! how I cher - ish thy fame! Then banish the thought, my
Cor.
own no-ble Knight, Shall re-turn in despite of the foe, What
f
Ped.
*
joy when a - far his lov'd form greets my sight, And his bugles, his bu - gles their
cres. ed. accel.
ff poco. rall.
wel-come shall blow! What joy, what joy, what joy, ... when his
mf
cres. ed. accel.
Sf
rall.
p
Ped.
Ped.
Ped.
*

bu gles their welcome shall blow,　　What joy,　　　what

joy,　　　　what　joy, ... when his　bu - gles, his bu - gles　their

wel - come shall blow!

No. 3. *a.* The Responses. *b.* Recitative and Arietta.

"The Night hath fallen round us."

EVENING. Close of Vesper service in the chapel of the castle. Escobedo, the chaplain, with the women, and such retainers as have not followed Don Munio on his expedition.

SOPRANO.

ff

Si - cut e - rat, in prin-cip-i-o, et nunc et semper; et in

ALTO.

TENOR.

ff

Si - cut e - rat, in prin-cip-i-o, et nunc et semper; et in

BASS. CHORUS. *ff*

to!

f

Str.

Organ and wind Inst. *sfz* *sfz*

sæ-cu - la sæ-cu - lo-rum, A - - men.

sæ-cu - la sæ-cu - lo-rum, A - - men.

Escobedo.

ff

Do - mi - nus vo-

Str.

39

Yet ere we part, as is most meet and right, and as

Church, our voices let us raise in Vesper-song, in

Fl. Clar. Fag. Cor.

a tempo.

mf

a tempo.

song!

Cor. Solo.

mf

p

cres.

Allegretto Moderato. ♩. = 72.

dim.

All other tho'ts forsake, Let each his station take, Let ho-ly song awake in

ac - - cents sweet. To her .. let praise be giv - - en,

Who .. for our sins hath striv - en, Who, that we be . . . for-

giv - - en, Doth plead, doth plead for us. To

ber.... let praise be giv'n, Who... for our sins hath striv'n, Who, that we be forgiv'n, Doth

plead.... for us,.... Doth plead.... for us,.... A - - ve, A - - ve Ma-

ri - - - a! A - ve Ma-ri - - - - - - - - a!

No. 4. Chorus. "Ave Maria."

kindly face,   Our supplications deign to   hear,   A - - - -

hear, our supplications deign to hear,   A - -

kindly face,   Our supplications deign to   hear,   A - - ve, A - - -

A - ve, A - - - -

cres.   dim.

dim.   p   p

ve, A - - ve Ma - ri - - - a!   Bene - dic - ta! blessed maid!

ve, A - ve Ma - ri - - - a!   A

dim.

ve, A - - ve Ma - ri - - - a!

fl.   ob.

p

Ped.   *   Ped.   *

- ri - - a,   Et Be-ne-

- - ve · Ma-ri - a!

- - ri - - a!   B

Fl. Ob.

dic - - - tus! wond'rous birth of Christ, our Lord, of Virgin pure!   Through

Et Benedictus!

Et Benedictus! wond'rous birth of Christ, our Lord, of Virgin pure!   Through

cres.   f

tion came to earth, Thro' thee,His aid is ev - er   sure,   A -

                                                       f

                    cres.   sure,Thro' thee his aid is ever

                                                       f

ion came to earth,   Thro' thee,His aid is ev - er   sure,   A -

                                                       f

                                                       A ve,

Ped.   *

                    p

                 3

- - ve, A - - ve, Ma - ri - - - a!

                 3   p

- - ve, A - - ve Ma - ri - - - a!

                    p

- - ve! A - - ve Ma - ri - - - a!

                 3

- - ve! A - - ve Ma - ri - - - a!

                 3

                    p

When the hour of death shall come,

When the hour of death shall come,

In ho ra mor - tis, ... mortis nos - træ, in hora, in ho - ra

Cor, Clar.

Veolli, Fag.

Timp

Ped. *

Our troub - - les past, O pray for us, that by the

Our troub - - les past, O pray for us, that by the

mor - tis, . . . mortis nos - træ.

Cor, Fag.

Str.

pizz.

Timp.

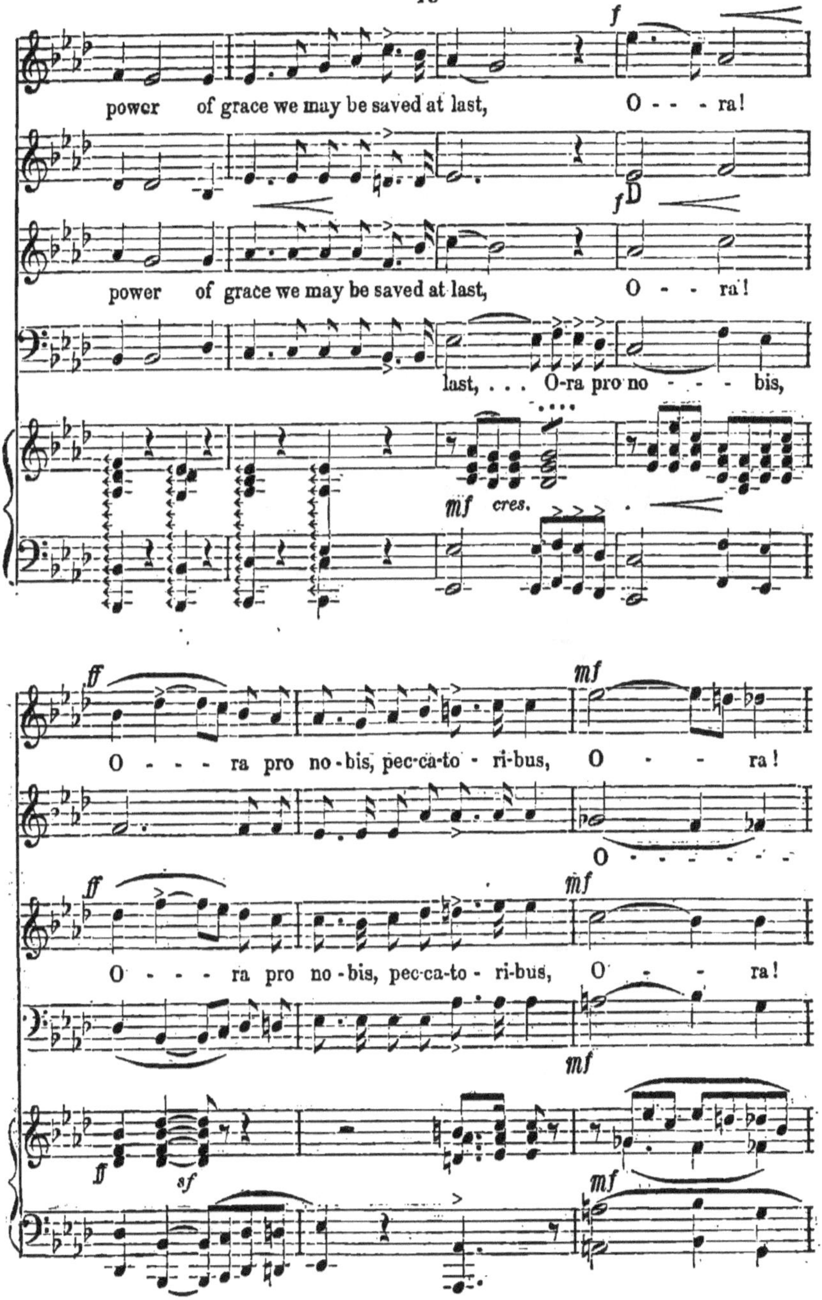
power of grace we may be saved at last, O - - - ra!
power of grace we may be saved at last, O - - - ra!
last, . . . O-ra pro no - - - bis,
mf cres.
O - - - ra pro no-bis, pec-ca-to - ri-bus, O - - - ra!
O - - - - - - -
O - - - ra pro no-bis, pec-ca-to - ri-bus, O - - - ra!
ff sf mf

No. 5. Recit. and Aria. "In the woods at early morn."

Morning in the Forest. Don Munio alone.

In circle wide, forth have I sent my vas-sals all. Aroused by loud halloo and blast of-horn, ere long the frighted stag hither his flight will

wend ; While 'neath this leafy covert will I take my stand, ex-

Allegro non troppo.

pectant waiting, till the game ap-pear.

In the woods . . . . . at ear-ly morn, sweet re-

sound . . . the forest voi - ces, Nature seems . . . . . . again new

born, and the heart ..... of man re - joi - ces, re -

rall.

joi - - ces! How the for - - est odors sweet Breathe their

p

perfumes on the air. Blest in - - fluence! thee my

con espress.

f *dim* Str. *p*

Ped. * R.H.

soul .... doth greet. Sooth - er of sor - row and of

Fag. Cor. Fag. Clar.

Strong of arm . . . . . and cool of nerve must the

trus - - - ty warrior be! Huntsman! thou too must not

swerve, When the game . . . approacheth thee, when the

game . . approacheth thee! Worthy then . of knightly skill is the

sport   the woods can show,   When peals the horn   from cliff and

hill,   and Echo   an - - - swers faint below.   Echo

answers,   Echo   answers,

faint . . . . . be - low,   Then how

sweet . . . at early morn   when re-sound . the woodland voices,   Nature

seems . . . again new born, . and the heart of man, the heart of man re-joi - - - -

ces.

No. 6. Recit. "But hark! what distant sounds!"

(The approach of the Moors.)

Don Munio. p RECIT. Moderato.

Tempo di Marcia ♩ = 100.

But hark! what distant sounds of

Accompaniment.

Clar.

Cor.

Fag.

Trombe.

RECIT.

Tempo.

music fall on my wond'ring ear!

mf Tempo.

Cor.

Str.

RECIT.

Agitato e cres.

In yonder vale, behold a cav-al-cade approaching, and women too among the

RECIT.

p

sf

Tempo.

RECIT,

train, all gaily deck'd as for a wedding feast! No hostile purpose can their

p

mf

fp A

footsteps guide, while yet their glitt'ring garb proclaims the Mos - lem! Ha! my good

sword! here shalt thou win most noble boo-ty, and a lord - ly ransom:

Sound, bugle, sound! Sound, bugle, sound! with gladsome news, my

vassals to re - call!

No. 7. CHORUS. "Birds! gaily singing o'er us."

(Female Voices.)

Females of the Moorish cavalcade, ringing as they journey.

Haste on . . . the path before us,   Raising . . . the joyous chorus, In

Haste on . . . the path before us,   Raising . . the joyous chorus, In

o'er us,   Haste on . . . the path before us, Rais - ing the cho - rus in

praise, in praise   of Love!   Ere   fall the shades of night.

praise, in praise   of Love!   Ere   fall the shades of night.

O may the marriage rite, Two faithful hearts unite, Sing praise to

O may the marriage rite, Two faithful hearts unite, Sing praise to

Un - til . . . our journey's end, Free - ly . . . our songs we spend, In

Un - til . . . our journey's end, Free - ly our songs we spend, In

journey's end, Free - ly our songs we spend, our songs we spend, In

praise of Love! Thus, safe from ev'ry

praise of Love! Thus, safe from ev'ry

praise of Love!

prize,   and win   the prize!

. . . the prize, and win . . . . the prize!

prize,   and win   the prize!

No. 8. Chorus. "Down with the Moslem!"

Don Munio's Retainers make their appearance from all sides, surrounding the Moors.

Down, aye! Down with the Mos-lem, the ha-ted, detest-ed! No

long - er shall thus our fair land be infest-ed! On warriors all! Draw the

sword! bend the bow! For God and Castile! See yon - der the foe! See

2nd. TENOR.

SOPRANO.

THE MOORISH WOMEN. Woe! Woe! ut - - ter woe!

ALTO.

A

yonder the foe, . . . See yonder the foe!

poco dim.

our jour - ney de-tect - ed; By blood - thirsty men is our

progress arrest - - - - - - ed! All the

hopes, fond - ly raised, in the dust are laid low, And

cres.

cap-tives are we to our bit-terest, bit-ter-est foe! *ff* Woe! Woe!

cres.

Constanza, *with Alto ad lib.*

ff

The Retainers.

Down with the Moslem! the hated, de-test-ed! No

ff

Abadil, *ad lib.*

Woe! ut-ter

Don Munio, *ad lib.*

Cap - tured the Mos-lem! the hat-ed, detested! The

B

cres. *sf* *sf* *ff*

Ped. *

mf

ut - ter woe! Our jour-ney de-tect-ed; By blood-thirsty men is our

longer shall thus our fair land be infest-ed!

woe!...... Our progress ar-rest

spoil it is ours, by our good swords arrest - ed!

mf

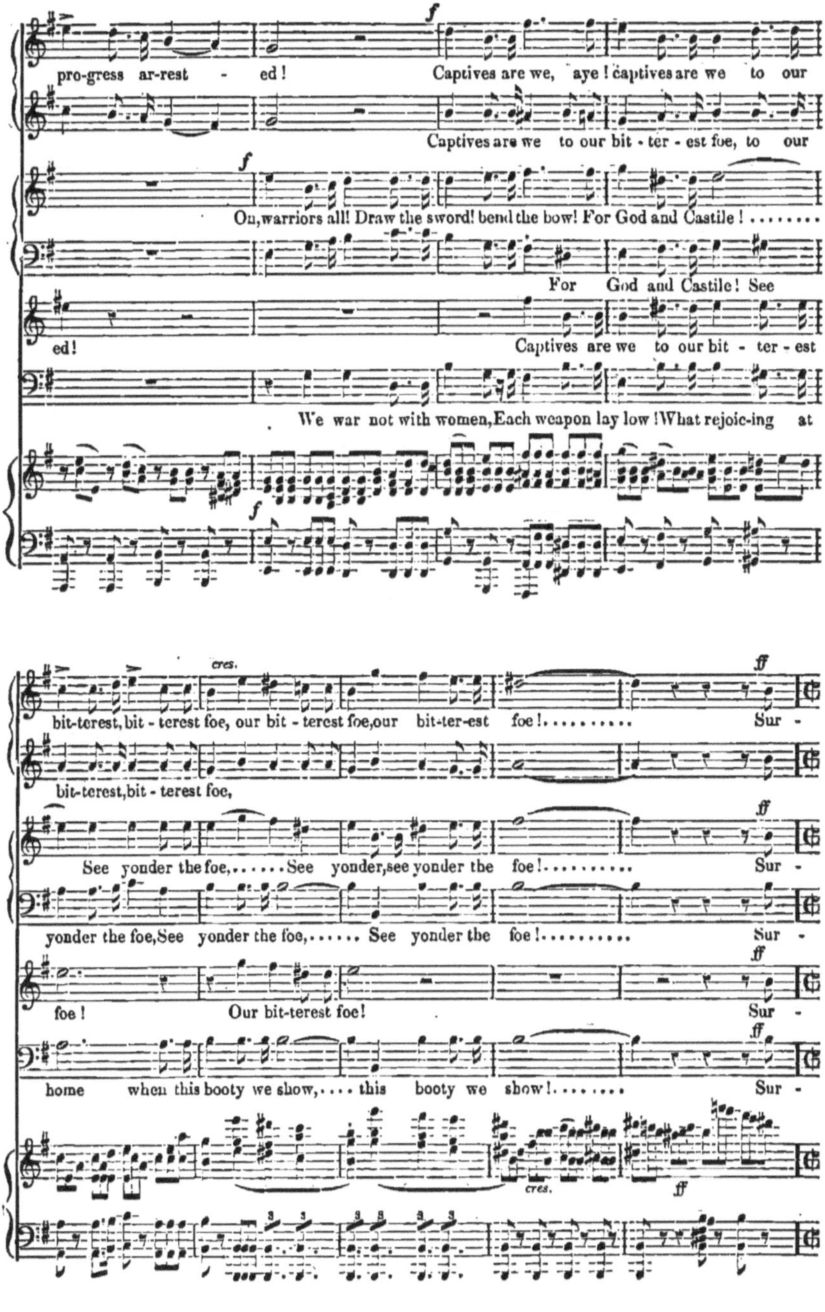
f
pro-gress ar-rest - ed! Captives are we, aye! captives are we to our
Captives are we to our bit - ter - est foe, to our
f
On, warriors all! Draw the sword! bend the bow! For God and Castile! ....
For God and Castile! See
ed! Captives are we to our bit - ter - est
We war not with women, Each weapon lay low! What rejoic-ing at
f
cres.
ff
bit-terest, bit - terest foe, our bit - terest foe, our bit-ter-est foe! .... Sur -
bit-terest, bit - terest foe,
ff
See yonder the foe, ... See yonder, see yonder the foe! .... Sur -
yonder the foe, See yonder the foe, ... See yonder the foe! .... Sur -
ff
foe! Our bit-terest foe! Sur -
ff
home when this booty we show, ... this booty we show! .... Sur -
cres.
ff

To whom can *we* turn? To whom can we

To whom can *they* turn? To whom 'can *they*

turn? . . . .

turn? . . . .

8va

Ped.

No. 9. Recit. and Aria, with Male Chorus.

"Unarmed, we yield·ourselves."

Abadil.

The Entreaty.

Un - armed, we yield ourselves to force of numbers!

Recitative.

f *dim.*

Tempo del No. 8. *poco rall. e dim.* But heard I not amid yon hostile

Recit.

cries, the name, the name of Mu-ni - o?

a tempo. *Recit.*

Don Munio.

'Tis even so, The knight who speaks with you is he : What wouldst thou?

p

Abadil.

Ar *lante non troppo.* ♩ = 69.

Hail, O no-ble Mu - ni - o!

On me a boon bestow, Known as a gen'rous foe, To

thee I plead, to thee I plead, Do . . not my suit disown,

When once our pur - pose known, In . . . thee I trust a - lone, To

Poco animato. ♩. = 96.

help our need. My name is

princely line, And this fair maid . . . of e - qual

To celebrate our marriage at a dis - tant shrine.

tan - do.

we this day . . our footsteps bent.

A

a tempo.

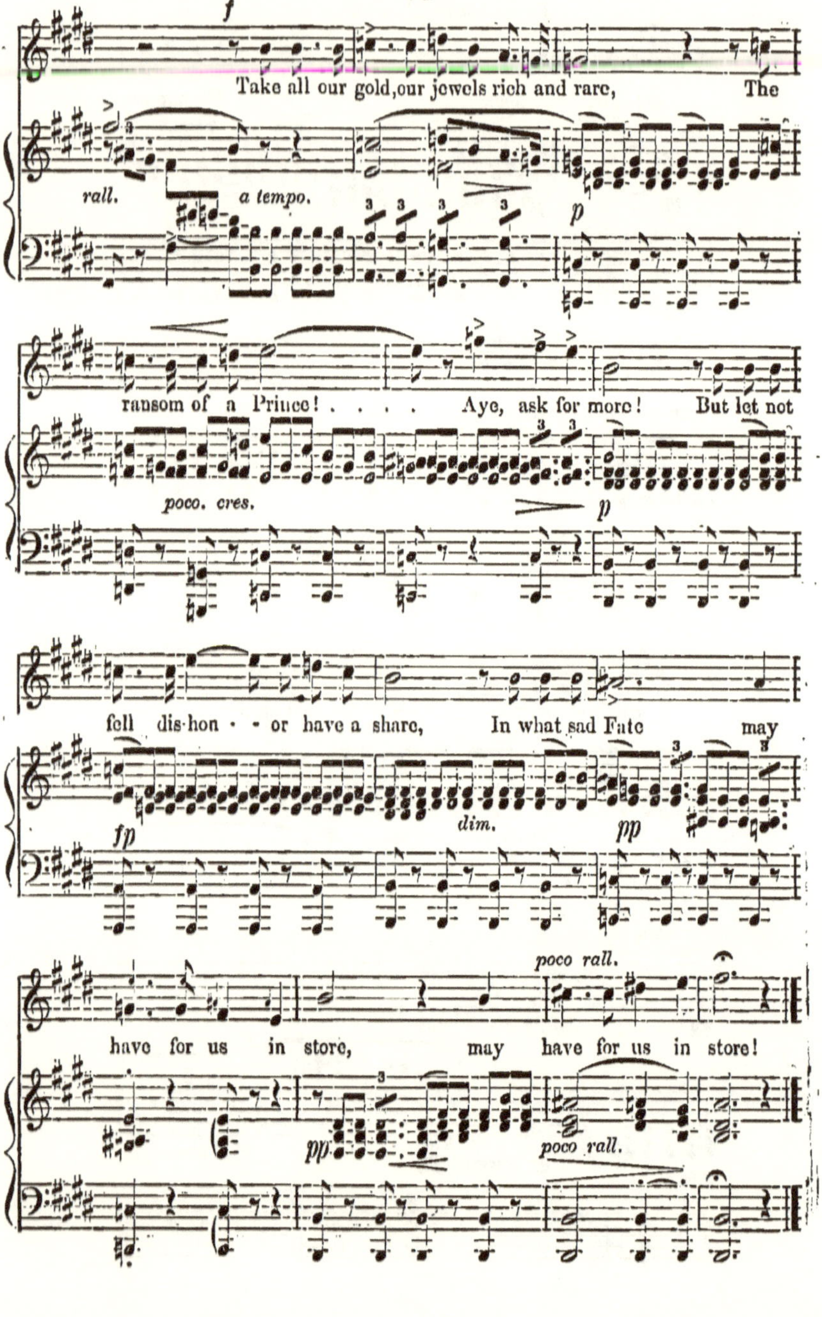
f
Take all our gold, our jewels rich and rare, The
rall.
a tempo.
p
ransom of a Prince! . . . . Aye, ask for more! But let not
poco. cres.
p
fell dis-hon - - or have a share, In what sad Fate may
fp
dim.
pp
poco rall.
have for us in store, may have for us in store!
pp
poco rall.

Tempo 1mo.

Then,   O no-ble Mu - ni - o!   On   me   a   boon   bestow,

TENORS 1 & 2.

ppp Staccato.
The bride is   pass - ing fair, Wit - ness her   great de - spair,

ppp BASS 1.

The bride is   pass - ing fair, Wit - ness her   great de - spair,

BASS 2.

ppp Staccato.

Don Munio's Retainers whispering together.
Tempo 1 mo.

pp

Be . . . . thou a   gen'-rous foe,   To thee I plead,   to

List   to   the   war-rior's tale, list   to   the

List   to   the   war-rior's tale, list   to   the

thee I plead, Do . . . not our suit disown, Now that our

tale! The sto - ry seem - eth true, What will Don

tale! The sto - ry seem - eth true, What will Don

sempre piano.

pur - - pose known, In . . . thee we trust alone, To

Mu - nio . do? Can aught a - vail?

Mu - nio do? Can aught a - vail?

cres.

help, ... to help, ... to help . . . our

cres.   *mf*

Can aught avail ?   Can aught avail ?   Can aught

cres.   *mf*

Can aught avail ?   Can aught avail ?   Can aught

cres.   *mf*

Ped.   ✻   Ped.   ✻   Ped.   ✻

need.

a - vail ?

a - vail ?

mf   *p*

No. 10. Recit. and Intermezzo. "Now God forbid."

The Ransom.

Now God for-bid, that I, a Christian knight, two loving hearts should force asunder, Tho' with no hos-tile purpose ye have come, But yet, as Mos-lems, captives of my sword, Hear

RECIT.

this, hear this, the ran - - som I will

mf

RECIT.

Andante con moto. ♩ = 76

take. Full fourteen days wi'hin my cas - - tle gate,

p

captive, yet not con-fined . . shall ye abide with me ; But

sempre piano.

there your nuptials will we cel - - e - brate, af - ter which time shall

p

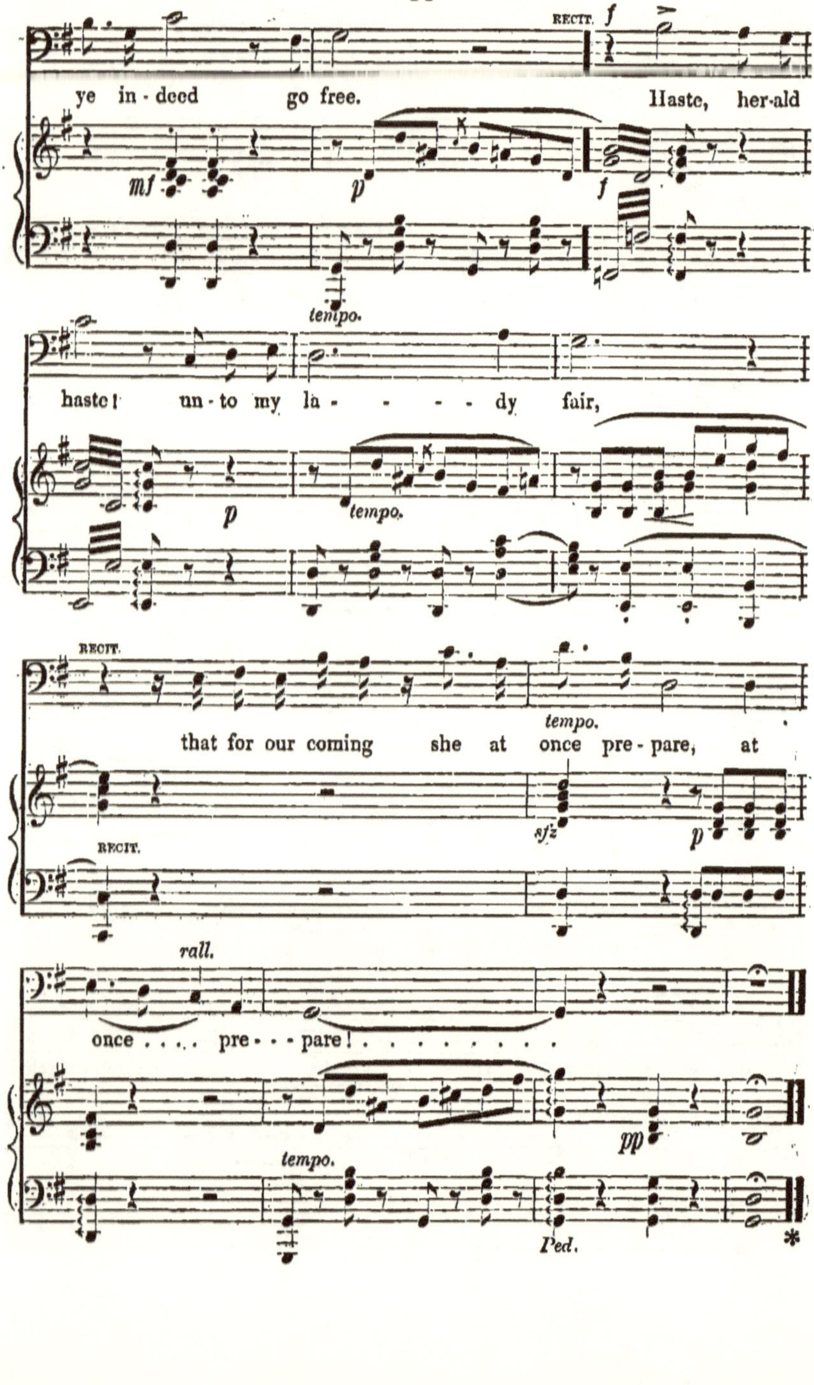

ye in - deed go free. RECIT. Haste, her-ald

haste! un - to my la - - - - dy fair,

that for our coming she at once pre - pare, at

once . . . . pre - - pare! . . . .

No. 11. Chorus. "Praise to Don Munio!"

The March to the Castle.

Allegro Vivace alla Marcia. ♩ = 104.

Praise to Don Mu-ni-o! What kindness to his foe, Doth the brave

Praise to Don Mu-ni-o! What kindness to his foe, Doth the brave

war - rior show, Let joy, let joy a - bound!

Constanza. (*Solo.*)

A - way ... with

war - rior show, Let joy, let joy a - bound!

Abadil. (*Solo.*)

A -

grief and fear! All sor - - rows disappear, Such knighthood we revere, Where'er 'tis

- way ... with grief and fear! All ... sorrows disappear, Such knighthood we re-

found, where - - e'er, where'er 'tis found!

- vere, wher - e'er .... 'tis found!

Trombe.

Sound, trumpets, sound! the

Sound, trumpets, sound! the

Ped. Ped. *

bri - dal train, the bri-dal train pre - ced - - ing, Sound, gen - tle

bri - dal train, the bri-dal train pre - ced - - ing, Sound, gen - tle

bri - - - dal train pre - ced - - ing, Sound, gen - tle

mf

lutes ! your tale of love, your tale of love re - veal - ing:

lutes ! your tale of love, your tale of love re - veal - ing:

Omit the 2d time.

Haste on your way! your banners wide, your banners wide displaying,

ban - - - ners wide displaying,

Haste on your way! your banners wide, your banners wide displaying, To Hymen's

ban - - - ners wide displaying,

Omit the 2d time.

Ped. ✻

To Hymen's feast, to Hymen's feast, let there be no de - lay - ing! Then

feast, ... to Hymen's feast, ... let there be no de - lay - ing! Then

To Hymen's feast, to Hymen's feast, let there be no de - lay - ing! Then

- bound!

- bound!

END OF PART FIRST.

8va bassa.

PART II.

No. 12. Recitative and Aria.

"The shadows deepen on the castle walls."

claim the coming of the night,   While on this terrace will I wait   to meet my

love.   Pa - tience, O longing heart !   Soon is thy trial o'er, and the glad morrow's

sun   shall see Constan - za thine !

grief full sore opprest. I think of thee, and tears come thronging, When thou art

present, I am blest. A

Waft her, o breeze, my tend'rest, tend'rest greeting; I

hear the chant from chap - - - el near. The hour draws

nigh...... for our glad meet - ing, O come, sweet love,......I'm waiting here. The hour draws

nigh.... . for our glad meet - ing, The hour draws nigh for our glad meeting, O come, O

No. 13. CHORAL. "Jesu, dulcis memoria."

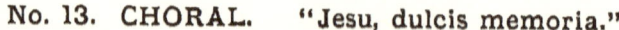

The Chapel Choir singing the Evening-Hymn.

Moderato.

SOPRANO.

Je - su, how sweet the ve-ry thought, That thou our hearts true joy hast brought:

ALTO.

Je - su, dul - cis me - mo - ri - a, Dans ve - ra cor - dis gau - di - a:

TENOR.

Je - su, how sweet the ve-ry thought, That thou our hearts true joy hast brought;

BASS.

Moderato. ♩ = 82.

ORGAN, OR WITHOUT ACCOMPANIMENT.

cres. *f* *dim.*

Hon - ey in sweetness is as naught, To that with which thy presence fraught. Jesu, the hope of

cres. *f* *dim.*

Sed su - per mel, et om - ni - a, E - jus dul - cis præ - sen-ti - a. Je-su, spes poe-ni -

cres. *f* *dim.*

Hon - ey in sweetness is as naught, To that with which thy presence fraught. Jesu, the hope of

cres. *f* *dim.*

cres.

pen - i - tent! How free to us thy grace is spent! Ah! who can doubt thy kind in - tent, To

ten - ti - bus, Quam pi-us es pe - ten - ti - bus! Quam bonus te quæ - ren - ti - bus, Sed

pen - i - tent! How free to us thy grace is spent! Ah! who can doubt thy kind in - tent, To

A

souls which thee to seek are bent, To souls which thee to seek are bent; O Je - su, ev - er -

quid in - ve - ni - en - ti - bus, Sed quid in - ve - ni - en - ti - bus? Sis Je - su, nostram

souls which thee to seek are bent, To souls which thee to seek are bent; O Je - su, ev - er -

B

more with thee, Be our reward thy face to see! And thro' a bright E - ter - ni - ty,

gau - di - um, Qui es fu - tu - rus præ - mi - um, Sit nos-tra in te glo - ri - a.

more with thee, Be our reward thy face to see! And thro' a bright E - ter - ni - ty,

Thine shall for aye the glory be, A-men, Amen, Amen, Amen, A - men!

Per cuncta sem - per sæ - cu-la, A - - - - men, A - - - men, A-men!

Thine shall for aye the glory be, A - men, A - men, Amen, Amen, A-men!

No. 14. Duet. "Dews of the Summer night."

The Castle Terrace. The Moorish Lovers.

down from on high.   Hark! in the grove to the nightingale

down from on high.   Hark! in the grove to the nightingale calling!   We....

Ob. Fag.

call - - ing!   We are a-lone,.... no list'ner is nigh,.... no list' - ner is

...... are alone,.... no list'ner, no list'ner is nigh,   We are alone, no list' - ner is

nigh!

nigh.   Con - stan - za! my loved one! my bride.... on the morrow! Fly

Fl. Clar.   Cor.

mf A   Fag.   p

swift... fleeting hours till the dawn shall appear! Dispell'd are the clouds which

erst threatened sor-row, The bright sun of Hope....hath removed ev'-ry fear, My

dear-est! my dearest! my thoughts art thou telling: O welcome the morrow which

makes me thy bride! These tears from mine eyes which now gent-ly aro well-ing, But

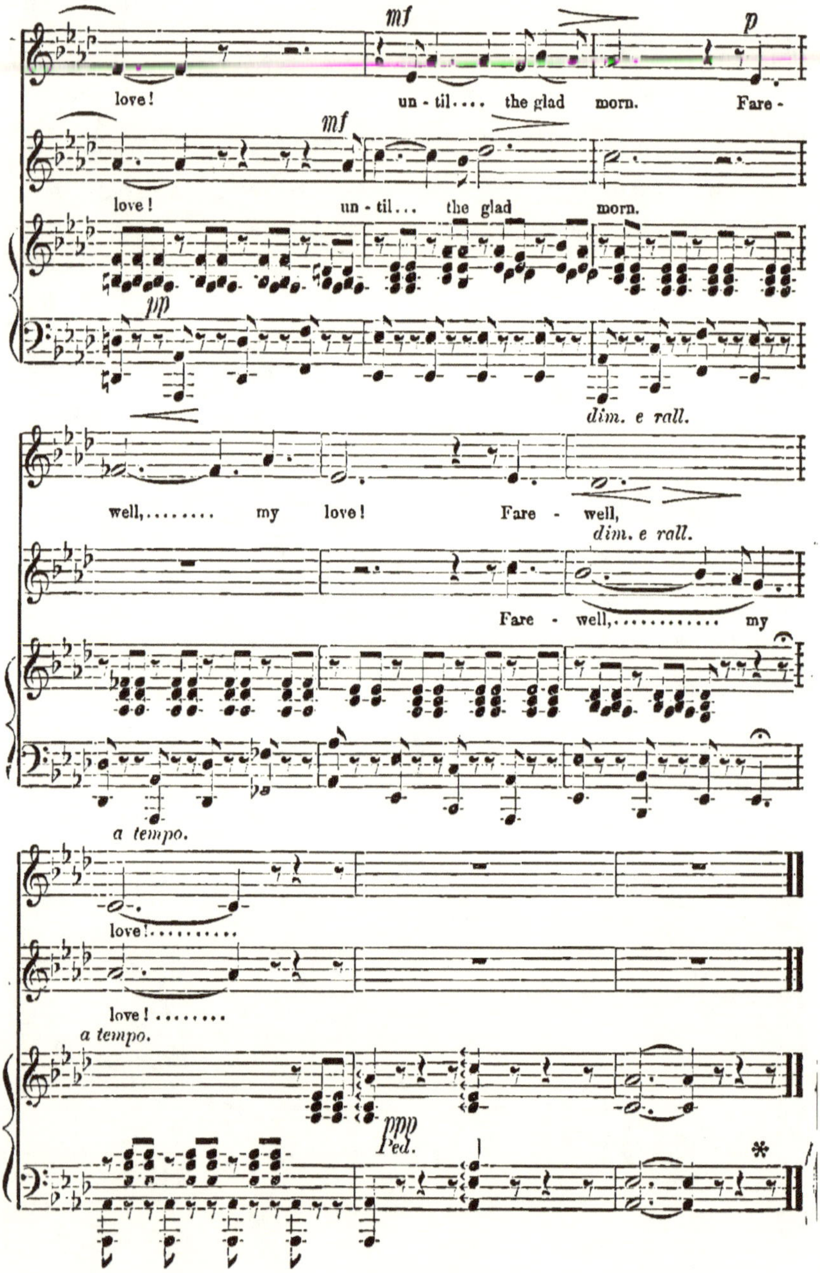

love!   un - til.... the glad morn. Fare-

love!   un - til... the glad morn.

dim. e rall.

well,........ my love! Fare - well,

dim. e rall.

Fare - well,........... my

a tempo.

love!.........

love!.......

a tempo.

ppp
Ped.

No. 15. Bridal Chorus. "United! united!"

The Festivities after the Marriage.

Mu-ni-o! U - ni - ted! u - ni - ted! their sor - rows re-qui - ted, Be-hold . . . the

U-ni - ted! u - ni - ted! their sor - rows re-qui - ted, Be-hold . . . the

hap - py pair . . ad - vance! U - ni - ted! u - ni - ted! Lo all are in-

hap - py pair . . ad - vance! U - ni - ted! u - ni - ted! Lo all are in-

vi - ted, To join in the maze of the merry, merry dance.

join in the maze of the

vi - ted, To join in the maze of the merry, merry dance.

join in the maze of the

mf Fl. Clar. Fag.

B

p TENORS.

Safe...... thro' life, secure from ill,

BASSES.

p

B Str.

Ped. Ped. * Ped.

vi - ted, To join in the maze of the merry, merry dance. All hail . . . .

vi - ted, To join in the maze of the merry, merry dance. All hail . . . .

Ped.   * *Ped.*

. . . to no - ble Muni - o!   All hail . . . . . to noble Mu - ni -o!

. . . to no - ble Muni - o!   All hail . . . . . to noble Mu - ni -o!

Ped.   *Ped.*   * *Ped.*

... All hail! . . . . . . All hail! . . . . . .

... All hail! . . . . . All hail! . . . . .

No. 16. BOLERO.

No. 17.   Quartett, without Accompaniment.

"IT IS THE LOT OF FRIENDS TO PART."

The Departure of the Moors.

Donna Maria.

It is the lot of friends to part; We meet as trav'llers of a

Constanza.

Abadil.

It is the lot of friends to part; We meet as trav'llers of a

Don Munio.

day: An interchange of heart with heart, and then, and then, ... each turns, and goes his

day; An interchange of heart with heart, and then, and then, ... each turns, and goes his

way, And then, and then each turns, and goes his way. O human

way, and then each turns, each turns, and goes his way.

life!........how short, how short,........thou art the joys of friendship well to learn, No sooner prized than forced a-

O human life! how short thou art, the joys of friendship well to learn.

O human life! how short thou art, the joys of friendship well to learn, No sooner prized than forced a-

part, How hard God's purpose to discern. And thus we part, We cannot know how we a-

part, How hard God's purpose to discern. And thus we part, We cannot know how we a-

gain, perchance, may meet, Whether opposed as foe to foe,.... or as a friend his friend doth

gain, perchance, may meet, Whether opposed as foe to foe,.... or as a friend his friend doth

greet,Then meantime let us hope, aye! let us hope and trust, that this our friendship may en-

greet,Then meantime let us hope, aye! let us hope and trust, that this our friendship may en-

No. 18. Duet. "Once more my royal master's call."

A Chamber of the Castle. Don Munio and Donna Maria.

Don Munio.

Once more, my royal

master's call, throughout the land by herald sped,

Summons to him his

calls,   I must obey, tho' now I feel th' approach of age, . .   This

once, And then with thee I'll stay, with ten - d'rest love   thy cares . . .   as-

Donna Maria.

O wilt thou promise?   Ah!

- suage.   Aye, indeed! But once more would I thee forsake.

why? ah, why?

That to the Ho - ly Land a pil - grimage I then might make.

poco. cres.

cres.

mf

dim.

p

mf

Ped. * Ped. * Ped. Ped. * Ped. Ped.

Allo. Vivace ma non Troppo.

Soon may the Moslem conquered be,

Then shall sweet Peace descend,

f

f

Soon may the Moslem conquered be, Soon may the Moslem conquered be,

Allo. Vivace ma non troppo. ♩ = 104.

mf

p

Then shall sweet Peace descend, And.. thro' our land, of foes made free.. Dire War, dire War shall have an

Then shall sweet Peace descend, And.. thro' our land, of foes made free,.. Dire War, dire War.. shall have an

end, ...   Soon may the Moslem conquered be,   Then shall sweet Peace descend,

end, ...   Soon may the Moslem conquered be,   Soon may the Moslem conquered be,

Ped.   * Ped.   * Ped.   *

Then   shall sweet Peace de-scend,   And .... thro' our land,   of foes made

Then   shall sweet Peace de-scend,   And .... thro' our land, of foes   made

free, Dire War,.... dire War .... shall have an end, ...

free, Dire War, ... dire War shall have .... an end, ...

Yes! thou must go, ... thy Sov' - - reign's call, I know.... thou must, thou

Yes! I must go! I must go! .... His Sov'reign's call each knight

must .... o-bey,.... Far .... better like a soldier fall, than

........should swift o-bey. .... Far .... better like a sol-dier fall, ... than craven here to

No. 19. Battle Hymn. *(Male Voices.)*
"Bring forth the clashing spear and shield."
The court yard of the castle. Gathering of Don Munio's Retainers.

A if it be our doom to lie out-stretch'd beneath some sullen sky,

A

Clar. Fag.

Ob. Clar. Fag.

mf

Receive our souls to thee on high, Great God of Bat-tle! Or if the vict'ry du-ly

mf

ff

cres.

Trombe. Corni.

won,   'Neath Palestine's resplendent sun. The pilgrim staff we'll bear: This we

dim.   p   B

dim.   p

p

swear! this we swear!............ The Sepulchre of

our dear Lord, That spot of all on earth adored, To seek be our first care. This we

swear! This we swear! Then

teach us how to choose the right.   Thine .... is the vict'ry, pow'r and might : Thro' thee a-

lone......we win the fight, Great God, great God of Bat · · · tle!

cres.

No. 20. "Requiem Æternam."

The Chapel of the Castle. Choir chanting the dirge for the dead,

f *Poco Vivace.*

- - mi - ne, Do-na e - is, do - na e - is-qui-em. Et lux per-

Do - mi - ne, Do - - - na e - is re-qui - em.

Do - ' mi - ne, do-na e - is, do - na, do - na e - is re-qui - em.

Do-na e - is, do - na,

dim. *Poco Vivace.* ♩ = 96.

pe - tu - a,.... et lux per-pe-tu - a, lu - ce-at, lu - ce-at e - - is.

Et lux per-pe - tu-a, lu - ce - at, lu - ce-at e - - is.

Et lux per-pe - - tu-n, Requiem æ-

No. 21. Solo with Chorus. "A year hath passed."

Escobedo, the Chaplain, addresses those assembled.

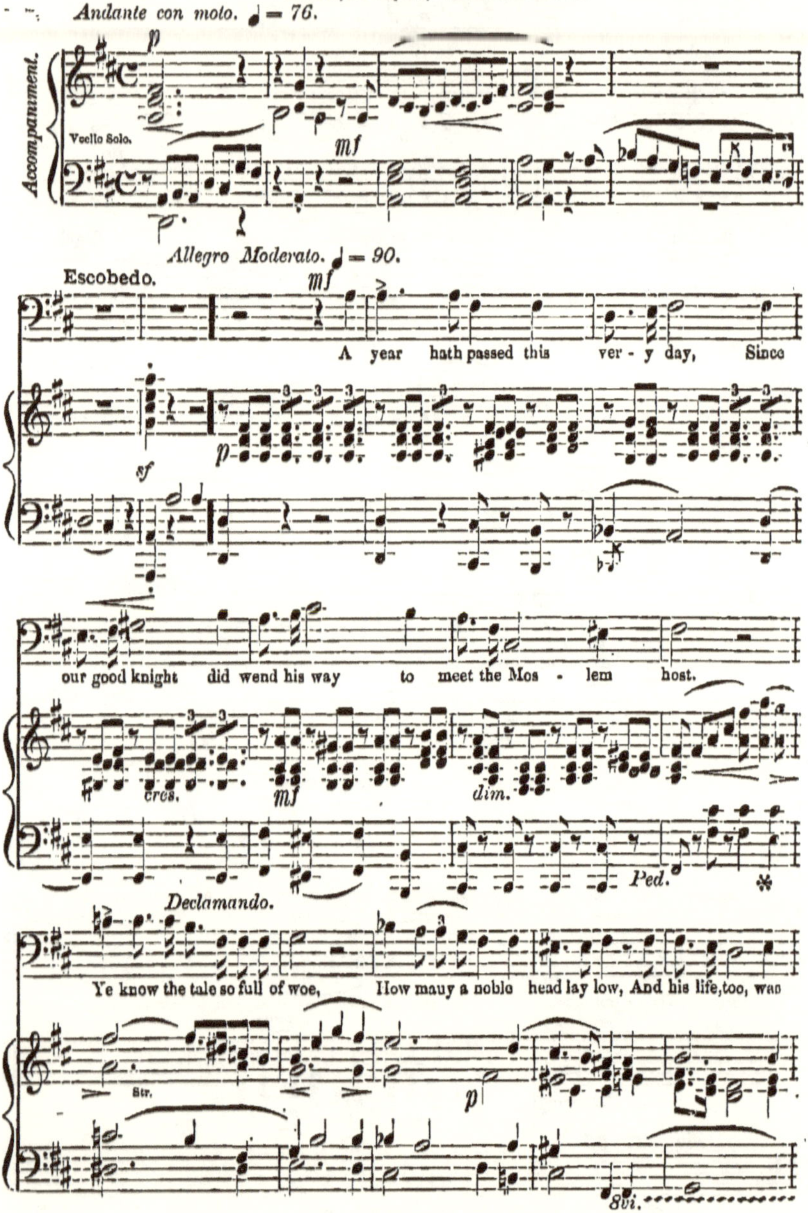

Andante con moto. ♩ = 76.

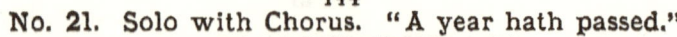

Allegro Moderato. ♩ = 90.

Escobedo.

A year hath passed this ver-y day, Since our good knight did wend his way to meet the Mos-lem host.

Declamando.

Ye know the tale so full of woe, How many a noble head lay low, And his life, too, was

N.B. (*Chorus remain seated during this and the following number.*)

A-las! his life was lost!....

A-las! his life was lost!....

lost. 'Twas passing strange that thus his end should

Clar. Fag. Cor. Vl.

come by hand of former friend, the no - ble A - ba - dil! With vizor

closed, all shining steel, naught did at first the fact re - veal, That Mu - ni - o was

Don Mu - ni-o was dead.

Don Mu - ni-o was dead.

dead.

Fruitless the grief of noble foe.

Fruitless the widow's tears and woe, for then 'twas all in vain: With

frequent masses for his soul, O may he soon .... attain the goal of

heavenly bliss, of bliss a - bove.

Now while we thus as-sembled

are, A messenger hath come, from far a wondrous tale to

tell; Give heed, and list with bated breath. Give heed, and learn how e'en in death, a knightly

No. 22. Recit. and Aria.

"Full many a long and weary league."

The message from Palestine.

Tempo di Marcia. Moderato.

Roderigo. *Recit.*

Full ma-ny a long and wea-ry league from Palestine, the sacred land I come.... Je-ru - - - sa - lem, the Holy Ci-ty, one year a - go a sight most strange be-held; to make it

known to you   am I com-mis - sion-ed.   One

Tempo.   rall.

Andante Cantabile. ♩ = 66.

summer eve,   as sank the sun,   While vesper bells...... to pray'r did call

Full   seventy warriors   one .. by one, Drew near   the Ho - ly

Sepulchre !   A   All dead-ly pale,   with vi - zor

raised, In si - lence mov'd their stead-y march, The crowd stood wondering, and

SEMPRE _pp_ STACCATISSIMO.

Cor.

Fag.

gazed— Towards the Ho - ly Se - pul-chre !

_mf_

dim.

Ped. * _Ped._ *

B

But I mys if right well did know the leader of this knight - ly

_p_

band, It was your own Don Mu - ni-o, Approached the Ho - ly

_p_

Ped. * _Ped._ * _Ped._

SOPRANO. *Poco Allegro.* cres.

What do we hear! Can this be true? Don Mu-ni-o was

ALTO.

What do we hear! Can this be true? Don Mu-ni-o was

CHORUS. cres.

Se - pulchre! What do we hear! Can this be true? Don

BASS.

What do we hear! Can this be true? Don Mu-ni-o was

Poco Allegro.

agitato.

seen by you, was seen by you!

seen by you, was seen by you!

Rodrigo.

Mu-ni-o was seen by you! They knelt within.... in silent prayer,

seen by you, was seen by you!

f *sf* C *dim.* *pp*

Ped. *

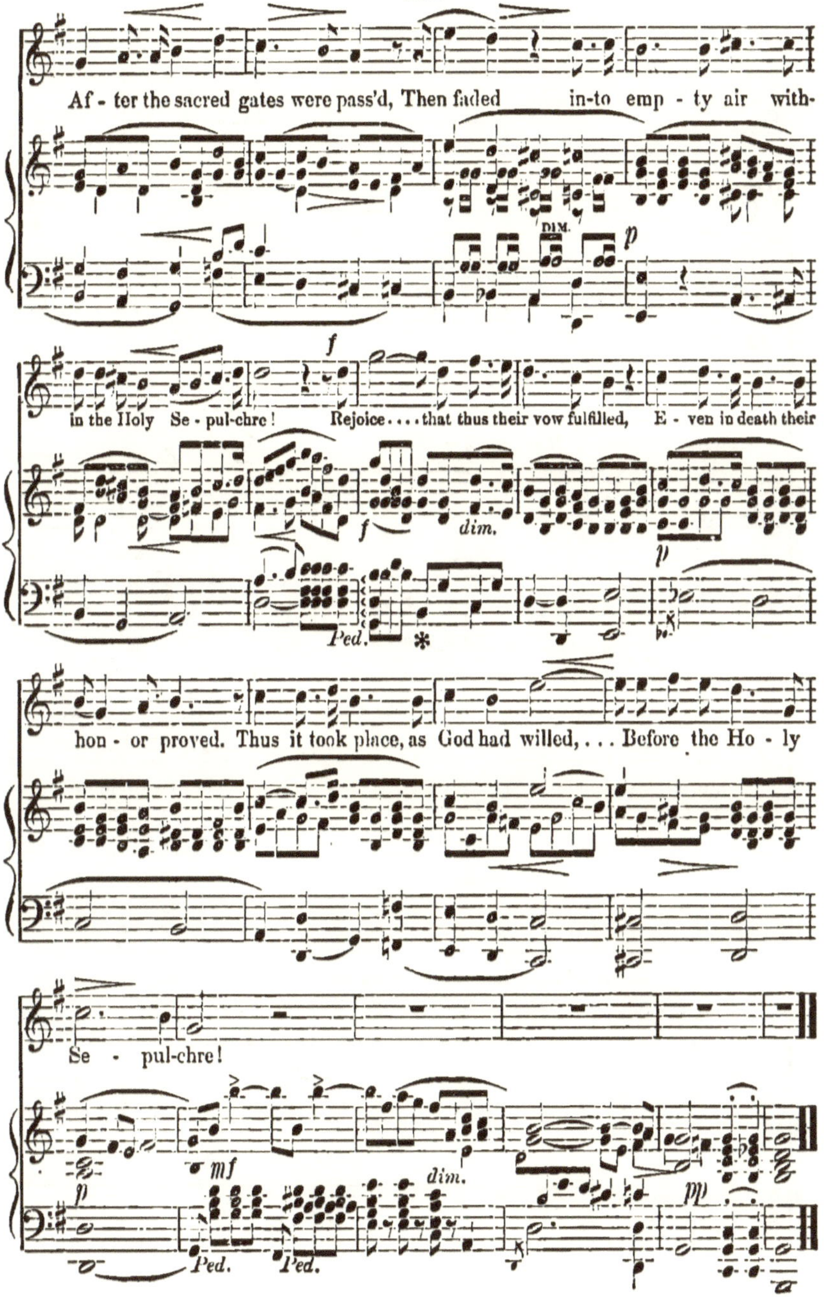
Af - ter the sacred gates were pass'd, Then faded in-to emp - ty air with-
DIM.
p
in the Holy Se - pul-chre! Rejoice . . . . that thus their vow fulfilled, E - ven in death their
f
f
dim.
p
Ped.
hon - or proved. Thus it took place, as God had willed, . . . Before the Ho - ly
Se - pul-chre!
p
mf
dim.
pp
Ped.
Ped.

No. 23. Finale. "In thankful hymns ascending."

Rap-ture super-nal, Bliss never ending, Now hath begun, Past the bright por - tal,

Rap-ture super-nal, Bliss never ending, Now hath begun, Past the bright por - tal,

Ser - aphs immor-tal, Prais - es are singing, Heav - en is won, ... aye! Heav'n is

Ser - aphs immor-tal, Prais - es are singing, Heav - en is won, ... aye! Heav'n . . . .

aye! Heav'n is